To Mum and Dad

First published in Great Britain 1986 by
MACMILLAN CHILDREN'S BOOKS
A division of Macmillan Publishers Limited
London and Basingstoke
Associated companies throughout the world

British Library Cataloguing in Publication Data
Higham, Jon Atlas
Aardvark's picnic
I. Title
823'.914 [J]   PZ7

ISBN 0-333-42822-6

Typeset by Universe Typesetters Ltd
Printed in Hong Kong

AARDVARK'S PICNIC

Jon Atlas Higham

MACMILLAN
Children's Books

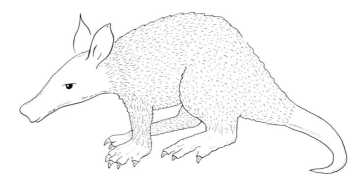

An aardvark is an animal that lives in Africa.

Aardvarks sleep in large burrows in the ground. They come out at night to search for ants, which they dig out with their large claws and then scoop up with long sticky tongues.

They look very much like pigs (aardvark means 'earth pig' in the Afrikaans language) and they have big ears so that they can hear well. They are a yellowy-brown colour and have long tails.

This story is about Aardvark who invites his friends to a special ant-picnic. But where are the ants?

Perhaps you can help Aardvark find them.

Aardvark woke up with a start. "Is that the time?" he said. "I'd better get a move on!" And he jumped out of bed.

It was to be a special occasion. He had invited his aardvark friends to an evening picnic (aardvarks have their breakfast in the evening because that's when they get up) and he hadn't even prepared the ant-paste sandwiches. Or the ant salad. Or the chocolate ant rolls. He would have to hurry.

Aardvark cut the bread and spread the butter;

he washed the salad and chopped the onions;

and then he hurried into the larder to fetch the ants.

But when he got there the ants had gone!

Where could they be? He hunted high,

he hunted low, but the ants were nowhere to be seen.

"Oh dear!" he said looking at the clock, "I shall have to find some ants along the way."

So he packed up his picnic basket and hurried out of the house.

He had gone a short way when he met the apes.
"Hello, Apes," said Aardvark. "I need some ants for my picnic. Do you know where I can find some, please?"

"I don't know about ants," replied the first ape.
"But bananas are good," added the second.
"And they would be nice to have on a picnic," said the third ape.

Aardvark thought that bananas didn't taste like ants, but the apes were his friends so he invited them along, and they all set off with Aardvark.

As they went along Aardvark looked for ants and listened for ants. But there was nothing.

When they reached the river they saw that Crocodile was cooking a meal.

"Hello, Crocodile," said Aardvark eagerly. "Are those ants you are frying? We need some for our picnic."

"Ants?" said Crocodile. "Why, of course not. They are delicious home-made fishcakes. Just right for a picnic."

"I suppose so," said Aardvark, wishing they had been antcakes.

"If you'll help me to look for ants on the way, you can come with us."

And off they went.

Soon they met Toad sitting on a rock. He was catching flies and dipping them into a large pot of honey. Aardvark looked at him hopefully.

"No, no," said Toad. "These are flies, not ants. No ants around here – just lots of flies. But why don't I bring some of my honey and join your party? Flies and honey are particularly nice for a picnic."

Aardvark would rather have had ants and honey, but as Toad was his friend he said, "What a good idea. Bring your honey and off we go." And all the way Aardvark kept looking for ants.

As they passed through the jungle they saw Snake.

"I hear you're having a picnic," he hissed (Snake always seemed to know everything that was going on).

"Why, yes," replied Aardvark, "and we've got bananas and fishcakes and honey, but no ants. Do you have any ants, Snake?"

"I'm afraid not," hissed Snake. "I eat eggs. Why don't you take some for your picnic?"

"How very kind of you," said Aardvark (although he didn't like eggs at all), "and you must come along too."

So Snake slithered off the tree and followed along behind the others.

When they came to the edge of the jungle they met Elephant.

"Hello, hello, hello, what's going on here?" said Elephant in a deep voice.

Aardvark looked at Elephant's long trunk and wondered if he used it for scooping up ants. He explained everything, right from the beginning.

"Don't worry," said Elephant. "I'm sure your friends won't miss the ants if you take some of these delicious crunchy leaves for your picnic."

"Leaves?" replied Aardvark, who was disappointed that Elephant didn't eat ants. "Why, of course. Would you carry them in your trunk for us, please? My friends will be waiting at the picnic site."

"Oh dear, oh dear, what a mess," thought Aardvark as he hurried on behind the others. "Where could I have put those ants?"

His hungry friends were waiting for him at the picnic site.

"Hello," said one of them. "What a nice surprise! You didn't tell us about all your friends. I hope there are enough ants to go round!"

"That's just the problem," said Aardvark. "I couldn't find *any*!"

"But what are all those things crawling out of your basket, then?" they said.

Aardvark couldn't believe his eyes.

"Why, of course!" he cried. "*That's* where I put my ants!"

All the animals laughed and cheered, and the aardvarks were delighted.

"Let's not waste a minute longer," said Aardvark. "On with the picnic!"

It turned out to be the best picnic they had ever had.

The apes ate the bananas, with a little of Toad's honey.

Crocodile had his fishcakes, also with a little honey.

Snake tried honey and boiled eggs.

Even Elephant had a leaf-and-honey sandwich.

And Toad helped everyone by spreading the honey for them.

As for the aardvarks, after the ant sandwiches, ant salad, and chocolate ant rolls they just couldn't eat another ant!